Not Yet, Zebra

Lou Kuenzler   Julia Woolf

ff
_____

FABER & FABER

To **A**ndrew - for tea and
wise words - **L.K.**

For Kate
J.W.

First published in the UK in 2018,
First published in the USA in 2018,
by Faber and Faber Limited,
Bloomsbury House, 74–77 Great Russell Street,
London WC1B 3DA

Text © Lou Kuenzler, 2018
Illustrations © Julia Woolf, 2018

PB ISBN 978–0–571–32976–2
HB ISBN 978–0–571–34288–4

1 3 5 7 9 10 8 6 4 2

The moral rights of Lou Kuenzler
and Julia Woolf have been asserted.
A CIP record for this book is available
from the British Library.

Annie said to the animals,
"Please stand in a line.
I'm painting my **alphabet**.
Come one at a time!

"First Aardvark and Bear, and Crocodile too.

"Not yet, Zebra. I'm not ready for you.
You're not the one I want to see.

Z comes at the end. We've only reached D.

"Now Dog and Elephant and ...

"Zebra, please think.

You are **NOT** Flamingo. You are not even pink!

"I need Gorilla and Hamster and . . .

What did I say?
Not yet, Zebra. Please go away!

"Now **I**guana.

Then **J**ellyfish.

"Then **K**angaroo.

"And **L**ion and **M**onkey must have a go too.

"N is quite tricky...

"But you're **DEFINITELY** not **N**ewt ...
I know you're just Zebra wearing a suit!

"O is for ... Oh no!

"Zebra, not yet!
Don't you know your alphabet?"

Annie sighed and said firmly, "**O**ctopus is **O**.
Stop pulling her legs and **PLEASE** let her go!

"**P**anda, **Q**uail, **R**hinoceros, come along through.
Let **S**nake slither in and ... Zebra, just **SHOO!**

"I know Tiger is stripy...
but he's not black
and white!

And Unicorn
CERTAINLY
doesn't look right.

"You can't mess about with the **ABC**.
We're still not at **Z**, we've only reached **V**...
Vulture and **W**alrus, please step forward next.

Now does anyone's name contain an X?

"Not yet, Zebra.
You are not FoX.

Don't be so naughty.
Let him out of that **box!**

"Go away, Zebra! Let **Y**ak have his turn.
When are **you ever** going to learn?

"Now who do I need? I am right at the end . . .

"Ah, yes!" Annie cried.
"Where's **Z**ebra, my friend . . . ?

"Where has he got to?" Annie looked all around.
But Zebra just simply couldn't be found.

"Strange!" Annie wondered,

"Was it something I said?

I can hear snoring.

Oh no, he's in ...

"...BED!"

A a
B b
C c
D d
E e
J j
K k
L l
M m
R r
S s
T t
U u